D0455129

This notebook is dedicated to
better-than-new
Shelah

Well, I can give myself a prize, can't I? →

PRIZE WINNING

SIMON & SCHUSTER BOOKS FOR YOUNG READERS
An imprint of Simon & Schuster Children's Publishing Division
1230 Avenue of the Americas, New York, New York 10020

Sorry! Same old Yakkity shmakkity. →

Copyright © 1999 by Marissa Moss

First Simon & Schuster Books for Young Readers edition, 2007

Book design by Amelia
(with help from Jessica Sonkin)

No technology involved!

now with secret ingredients — so secret, they're in code! →

The text for this book is hand-lettered. ✓

Manufactured in China
4 6 8 10 9 7 5 3

CIP data for this book is available from
the Library of Congress.

ISBN-13: 978-1-4169-0908-8
ISBN-10: 1-4169-0908-7

0318 SCP

EASY OPEN PACKAGE

↑ No batteries necessary!

Which is better — smiling with your mouth open or closed?

This is me, Amelia, trying to look like a movie star. Instead it looks like I've got popcorn stuck between my teeth. I don't want to <u>be</u> a movie star, but it'd be nice to look like one. Cleo, my jelly-roll-nose sister, is always practicing her smile in the mirror. And she practices her "looks."

All her "looks" look goofy to me. No matter what she does to her face, she still looks like Cleo (and sounds like her and acts like her).

Cleo's dramatic look

Cleo's sultry look

I didn't used to think about my face. It was just my face, but now I can't help noticing it — and wishing it were different.

Cleo's I-know-something look

Cleo's perky look

Cleo's ya-gotta-be-kidding look

Cleo's sweet look

Cleo's sweet look (The difference between "sweet" and "perky" is the slightly open mouth)

Charisse dropped her pencil and I picked it up. It even has her teeth marks on it because she chews on pencils. I would write with it, but that would wear it down and I want to keep it!

It's all because of this new girl in school. Her name is Charisse, and everything about her is PERFECT, starting with her name. Charisse sounds so elegant and beautiful.

Charisse looks like the drawings of princesses I made when I was little.

long blond hair

perky button nose

shimmery earrings

shiny pink lips — she wears lip gloss!

naturally, she's tall, too, not the shortest kid in the class like me

She's already amazing with a name like Charisse and a princess face, but she's even _more_ wonderful than that. She used to live in London and she has a British accent, so even her voice is beautiful. At recess everyone crowds around her to ask questions about living in London and stuff like that.

I wish she would be my friend, but she hasn't said one word to me so far, not even hello.

How to draw a princess in 3 easy steps:

Put arms behind her back so you don't have to worry about drawing hands.

Use pink!

Make a big skirt to cover legs and feet. ②

Add princess hat and long flowing hair — yellow, of course.

Now all you need is the delicate princess fa

Add bows, frills to dress to make more princes

①

Charisse even has a cool backpack — it's like a briefcase with straps so you can wear it on your back. →

She calls it a satchel. I love that word — "SATCHILL."

Two :exciting: things happened at school today. Charisse bumped into me when I was behind her in line for the drinking fountain. It was just a little bump, but she said, "Oh, pardon me!" and looked RIGHT AT ME! I wanted to say something back, but I was so surprised that she actually talked to me that I didn't know what to say. So I just got a drink of water.

why do I always think of the right thing to say when it's too late to say it?

Why didn't I say, "That's all right" or "No problem" or "Excuse me" or SOMETHING!?

The second exciting thing was that Ms. Busby has a special project for us — so special it's not even on school grounds, it's on a construction site! Some business guy bought some property to build a strip mall on, but when the bulldozers started clearing the land, they found some ancient Native American artifacts! Now some archaeologists are excavating, but the owner is only giving them a month to find things because he's in a hurry to build. So we get to help!

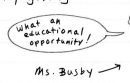

What an educational opportunity!

Ms. Busby →

Ms. Busby taught us a little about digging today. You don't use big tools like this one.

You have to dig really carefully a sift through the dirt like you're panning for gold.

Two people hold the handles and shake. Dirt falls through the mesh screen — treasure (and rocks) stays behind.

The archaeologists asked for volunteers, and Ms. Busby thought it would be verrrry educational. I just think it will be fun! It'll be like digging for dinosaur bones or buried treasure. I hope I find something.

Naturally, everyone wants to be Charisse's partner on the dig. (Doesn't that sound cool — we're working "on the dig"!) Everyone except Carly, that is. She still wants to be my partner. I want to be hers, too, but it'd be really GREAT if I got to work with Charisse.

Each pair of partners will be responsible for their own little square of land — it's a BIG job!

a real mystery spot

Everyone's excited. Well, almost everyone.

Carly →

me ←

→ Charisse

This will be like digging up the past!

Imagine — we get to help real scientists!

What's all the fuss about? Playing in dirt doesn't sound interesting to me.

One reason Charisse thinks the dig is no big deal (no big-dig deal) is because in England, they have tons of historical stuff above ground. You don't even have to look for it, it's just there.

kitten Pocket Pet ↓

pocket fawn ↓

pocket badger ↓

pocket fox ↓

pocket mouse ↓

Charisse might not be impressed with the project, but everyone is definitely impressed with _her_. She started a new trend when she came to school with a little furry toy animal in her shirt pocket. She says they're very popular in England. They're called "Pocket Pets."

pocket goat ↓

She must have a zillion of them because every day she brings a new one. You can't find them in this country, but kids are bringing small stuffed animals (usually bears) and calling them Pocket Pets, too.

Carly thinks everyone is acting stupid. You don't

pocket turtle ↓

see _her_ wearing a teddy bear in _her_ pocket. I don't have any animals small enough to fit into a pocket, so I'm not part of the trend either. Carly thinks it's because I'm on her side, but if I had a tiny bear, I'd DEFINITELY bring it.

Carly passed me this note. ↓

ocket onkey ↓

Can you believe how many people brought bears today? I'm glad you're not just a zombie follower like they are!

I am a zombie follower. I'm just not good at it. Would Carly still like me if she knew?

At lunch I sat with Carly, but I kept watching Charisse.

zombie look

Amelia. Amelia! AMELIA!! Aren't you listening? And WHAT are you gawking at?

Today we started working at the excavation — and CHARISSE IS MY PARTNER! I couldn't believe my luck! Carly got stuck with Brandon (who drives me CRAZY the way he's always jiggling his foot), but she said she felt sorry for *me* getting Charisse. I didn't say anything.

This is going to be totally great. I'll get to do all this neat stuff, and Charisse will have so much fun working with me, she'll want to be my friend.

Our first job is to sift dirt in these big mesh trays. If we show we're careful and responsible, then we can actually dig.

The dig site is like Mom's lasagna — each layer will have things from a different time period, with the more recent stuff on top. (Come to think of it, sometimes Mom's lasagna tastes prehistoric.

Dig into the dig!

CHEESE or dirt from today

SAUCE or dead leaves, bottle caps, dirt from last decade

VEGETABLES or stuff from last century

NOODLES or stuff from 500 years ago

CHEESE or stuff from 1,000 years ago

SAUCE or stuff from 2,000 years ago

VEGETABLES or stuff from 5,000 years ago

NOODLES or prehistoric stuff — we won't get this far!

what we're looking for now:

We're on the top layers of the lasagna, so we won't find really old stuff yet.

↑ old coins

↗ glass beads

metal tools and knives ↓

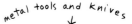

I don't know how we'll have time to get all the way back to 6,000 B.C., but that's what the archaeologists hope to reach. It's ~~wierd~~ ~~weird~~ ~~wierd~~ ~~weird~~ ~~wierd~~ weird to see time frozen solid this way. If I think about it <u>too</u> hard, it makes me dizzy!

↑ YIKES! Who invented this word anyway?!

I'd be happy just finding something from the days of the Gold Rush, but Carly wants to find something Native American, not pioneer stuff. Charisse doesn't care about finding anything. She says the whole thing is a big bore. Maybe <u>I'm</u> what's boring her. I need something to spice myself up!

chili sauce to give you some pizzazz!

Too bad there aren't condiments for people.

pickles to → give you some relish!

lemon to give you some zest! (Get it? Lemon peel — lemon zest!)

And ↗ I don't mean salt and pepper!

Today I thought of a great way to give myself some OOMPH! At dinner I tried out my ˙new˙ British accent. I asked Cleo to "puh-lease pawss the pun-tah-toes."
   "Soitenlee, yer majesty," she said. Cleo couldn't be elegant if she tried. She's stuck with the genetic makeup of a Cleo. I may not be Charisse, but I'm trying to be the next best thing. From now on, I'm asking everyone to call me "Ah-mell-ya," not "A-meal-ia." That way I'll sound good when people are talking to me and when I'm talking to them.

dumpy
toe-may-toe

ordinary
poe-tay-toe

elegant puh-tah-toe

glamorous
tuh-mah-toe

If you say "Ah-mell-ya" right, you pooch your lips forward instead of stretching them.

↑ right

wrong! ↗

Mom's the worst. She never remembers <u>anything</u>. No matter how many times I correct her, she keeps saying my name wrong. I'm working on my signature, too. I need a new one to match the new way I'm saying my name.

Well, I named you, so I should know how to pronounce it.

Mom with her exasperated look

too plain
↘ *Amelia*

too much like my old signature
Amelia ↓

Amelia
↑ I like the A, but the rest is too ordinary.

→ eeeAmelia
The problem with this is that making all the curlicues takes waaay too long.

Amelia
pretty fancy how the big A and little a connect

When I told Carly to call me "Ah-mell-ya," she said she would if I would call <u>her</u> Carly. I said I <u>was</u> calling her Carly. "No, you're not," she said. "You're saying Collie, like I was a dog or something." I told her it was just my accent, I couldn't help it. She got mad and said I could, too, help it since I didn't have an accent like that yesterday. Some people just don't appreciate self-improvement.

VOICE PAGE

I thought voices didn't matter, but they <u>do</u>. People's voices match their personalities. I <u>need</u> a good voice.

Cleo's voice is like a sponge scrubbing a pot.

Mom's voice is like dark chocolate.

Nadia's voice is like walking on fresh snow.

Charisse's voice is like water pouring into a tall glass.

Carly's voice is like warm flannel pajamas.

Gigi's voice is like pancake syrup.

Ms. Busby's voice is like crackling autumn leaves.

Leah's voice is like wool thread.

My voice is like — ? It's hard to hear your own voice — I hate listening to mine when it's recorded because it doesn't sound like me.

some bigger things we could find

We're deep in the lasagna now!

baskets (or parts of baskets)

whalebone tools

carved bowls

Now we don't even have a month to finish the excavation! The owner says he has to start construction in ~~3~~ weeks! How much work can we do in that time? We'll never even get past this century!

Some environmental and historical groups are protesting the building plan. They want the archaeologists to have time to find everything that's here — but that could take years, <u>definite</u>ly longer than a few weeks!

Professor Vallejo → is in charge of the dig. She says our only hope is to find some important artifacts to show that this is a site worth exploring.

So far the oldest thing found (not by us) was a stone hook used for fishing that dates back about 500 years. Our job is to find more (and better) stuff.

Everyone worked really hard today. Each day counts, so we <u>have</u> to. (Well, <u>I</u> think we should — Charisse still thinks it's "all a big brouhaha." I don't know what a brouhaha is, but I wish she'd help me more. It's harder to shake dirt through a screen than I thought.

other things to look for ↓

stone tools (drills, spearheads, arrows, hooks) ↓

spoons or bowls made from horn ↓

The tools we're trying to find don't really look like tools to me. Then I think of someone from the distant future excavating our house and finding a bottle opener. It doesn't look like much of a tool either.

child's toy? ↑ dental tool? ↑ earring? ↑

I can't help wondering about the story behind the button. Who made it and who wore it and what was it on? Maybe it was used over and over again on a lot of people's clothes.

Brandon's button

Today was really EXCITING! Brandon found a button — a whalebone button! I haven't found anything, but knowing that SOMEONE has makes it feel like it's possible. TREASURE is definitely here. We just have to find it.

Brandon's smile was almost as wide as his face — I guess all that jiggling jiggled the button out.

Carly looked so proud of Brandon — I couldn't help it, I was jealous.

Now I think maybe Carly's the lucky one in terms of partners. Charisse is just SO SLOW. Maybe it's part of being elegant — she doesn't want to get her hands dirty or chip her pretty pink nail polish. Part of her slowness isn't her fault. Other kids are always stopping to talk to her. And sometimes she makes _me_ slow, too — I should be watching the screen carefully, but I'm watching Charisse instead. Just the way she holds her mouth and looks thoughtful is so cool. I wonder if I could _ever_ look like that.

If you don't think about your mouth, it just sits on your face, but you can control _how_ it sits.

Some people always have a slight frown.

Some people look like their mouth is stuck in the down position.

some have a look of slight amusement.

Some let their mouths drop open and look like fish.

I used to make fun of Cleo spending so much time arranging her face in the mirror, but now I'm doing it.

my excited, perky look ↓

my sophisticated I-know-that look ↓

my been-there, done-that look ↙

First I have to open my eyes WIDE and keep them that way (this is the hardest part). Every now and then I flare my nostrils (but not too much or I look like my nose is flapping its wings and getting ready for takeoff). I keep my lips barely parted, smiling juuust at the edges.

This is the face I use around Charisse, but so far she hasn't noticed.

For this look I have to narrow my eyes, which is not as hard as keeping them wide open at first, but gets really tiring. I keep one eyebrow raised (I'm still working on this part) and make my eyes look intelligent (I'm working on this, too). My mouth is curved into a smile on one side only (switching sides every now and then is O.K.).

This look shows how worldly and experienced I am, just like Charisse. My eyes are partly closed (but I can't look sleepy!) and my eyebrows are raised (I should say "arched"). My lips are closed but bunched together — I'm trying for a pouty look, but I don't want to seem froggish. I thought this was a highly successful look, but when I tried it on Carly, she asked if I had a stomachache or something.

Professor Vallejo is teaching us how to "read" a culture from the objects it leaves behind. I wonder if she could figure out who I am by looking at my room.

books— evidence of love of reading

markers, colored pencils, notebooks— signs of writing and drawing

traces of marshmallows stuck on the ceiling— sign of a curious ritual or cooking method

The bad part about looking in the mirror so much is that I don't even look like me to myself anymore. I used to just see me, Amelia, but now it's like I see a face that's not mine. I mean, I'm still me, but instead of feeling PART of my face, I feel APART from it. I hate that!

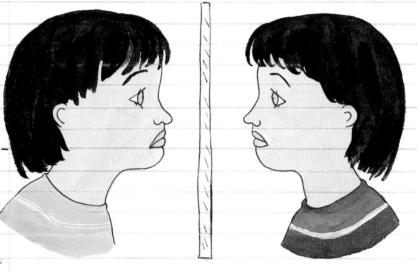

It's like hearing my voice recorded — my own face isn't familiar anymore. Instead, I keep noticing all the things I don't like about it — it's too round, my chin's too pointy, my ears stick out too much, and my hair just sits there. I suppose I should be grateful — at least I don't look in the mirror and see a jelly roll nose!

→ rainbow fingers

Now my fingernails look like M&M's and I keep wanting to eat them — they don't look pretty, but they DO look delicious!

Unfortunately, the polish doesn't change the <u>shape</u> or <u>length</u> of my nails, so instead of looking elegant, my fingers look stubbier than ever.

Today I tried nail polish. (Cleo's of course — I don't waste <u>my</u> money on that kind of junk.) But it didn't make me feel more glamorous like I thought it would. Instead, it was just distracting. I couldn't write or draw without noticing my nails, which got in the way of noticing what I was doing, so all my drawings turned out crummy and my handwriting was even worse than usual (hard to believe that it <u>could</u> get worse, but it <u>did</u>).

Maybe it doesn't matter if my drawings stink. I've been working so hard at getting Charisse to like me, I don't have much time left for making stories anyway. It's been a looooong time since I wrote a story in my notebook. Do I even remember <u>how</u> to write anymore? Do I have ideas worth writing about? Nail polish sure would make a boooring story!

I thought since I can't make myself tall or pretty, at least I could improve my fingernails, but nail polish just doesn't do it!

Nail polish looks <u>most</u> appealing in the cute little bottle — <u>not</u> on my hands.

UR#12 ME!

Dear Nadia,

Guess what? I'm changing my style so I'll be more, well, I'm not sure, but more ~~something~~. Don't worry, I'll still be your friend. I just need some pizzazz!

It's like this excavation we're working on. We're digging and sifting dirt to uncover old treasures. Me, I need to discover new treasures in myself. love, Amelia

Nadia Kurz
61 South St.
Barton, CA
91010

I wrote a postcard to Nadia about the new me and the archaeological dig.

Trying to add layers onto myself is making me feel like a lumpy lasagna.

cheese or accent

noodles or fingernails

sauce or expressions

I try to think of myself as getting closer to the perfect Amelia bit by bit, day by day. I just have to practice (my accent, my expressions, my nail-trimming and polish-wearing). I wonder how long it will take before it all feels normal to me? I'm hoping it's like learning a foreign language — it will just take time (and patience).

Unfortunately, at school today, Carly didn't appreciate all my hard work.

Will all this ever cook right and taste good?

What is with you these days? You're wearing nail polish?! Your sister sure is a bad influence! Good thing I only have brothers.

I don't want to hear about it!

Sometimes I don't know if it's Carly talking or that little voice in my head that criticizes what I do. Either way, I wish it would shut up!

At least the excavation is going well. Today we were even allowed to try digging, not just sifting. Because the things we're looking for might be small and fragile, we need special tools.

You DON'T use these!
↓

↗ spade   shovel ↗

You use these.
↓

↗ sharpened chopsticks

dental tools (open wide!) ↑   wooden putty knives ↑

To clear away dirt, we use:
↓

toothbrushes ↖

whisk broom ↗

paintbrushes ↗

I almost feel like an artist or sculptor using these things. I knew this excavation would be cool, but it's even cooler than I thought!

I actually like digging— it's almost like being back in kindergarten.
↓

↑ the sandbox

I haven't found anything so far that's historical or interesting, but I _have_ started a collection of cool rocks I've come across. Charisse doesn't like rocks any more than she likes digging (which is NOT AT ALL), but Carly likes my idea. She already has some great rocks and minerals at home, but she's finding more.

serpentine ↘

shale ↙

granite ↓

quartz ↘

Imagine an archaeological dig of Cleo's room. →

covered in
ancient sock
detritus →

trapped
in
neolithic
dust bunnies →

buried in
prehistoric
cereal
crumbs

I know my mood ring
is here somewhere.

I've been missing one
pink sock for aeons now.

Sealed in primordial ooze →

If I could excavate,
maybe I'd find all the
stuff she's "borrowed."

If I practice
archaeology at
home, maybe I'll get good enough at it to find something besides rocks.

FORTUNE TELLER

MIRACLE FISH

Nadia got my postcard, and she sent me this fortune-
teller fish. She said I don't need to change my style,
she likes me just the way I am (but Charisse sure
doesn't seem to!). Nadia said if I put the fish in the
palm of my hand, it will tell me about myself. (Good
thing it's not a real fish, all slimy and stinky, but
just a piece of veeeery thin plastic that's shaped
like a fish.)

the fortunate fish — I mean, fortune-telling fish →

I tried it and the fish's head and tail moved. Then the whole thing curled up. According to the wrapper the fish came in, that means I'm in love AND passionate! That's good — I think. At least it means I'm _not_ boring. But who am I in love with? The fish? Or does being in love with someone's accent count?

Charisse is getting annoyed that for all our work (well, _my_ work, because _she's_ not doing much), we haven't found anything yet. Today Max and Susie found part of a bowl carved out of horn or bone. Or maybe it's a cup. Whatever it is, they're <u>so</u> lucky!

It's amazing how much dirt you can look through in one day and still <u>not</u> find ANYTHING!

see, see, see, SEE, SEE!

Max was so excited, he ran up to every<u>one</u> to show off his treasure.

Professor Vallejo was very excited, too. She hopes the carving will help identify which tribe lived here. And the owner of the lot happened to show up just when Max was screaming, "Eureka, I found it!" Even _he_ came to take a look,

He didn't want to be impressed, but I could tell he was. I hope that means he'll give us longer to dig.

Now more and more kids are finding things. Will it _ever_ happen to me?

Raoul and Gabe found a clay pipe.

Lucy and Seth found an old glass bottle.

Jacqueline and Franny found a liberty head nickel.

I have the worst luck! Charisse hasn't noticed my accent or expressions OR nail polish. All she's noticed is that I'm a failure at digging. I thought being her partner would make her like me, but it's turning out to be just the opposite. I feel like I'm bad at EVERYTHING now! It's not even fun to collect rocks anymore — all I find is JUNK anyway.

My amazing discoveries
↓

a dirty plastic dinosaur →

a rusty screw ↘

ancient bottle cap (if you think last year is ancient) ↗

← a piece of broken tile, probably from a bathroom (how exotic!)

antique plastic button — what a beauty! ↗

When Carly's mad, it's like a storm cloud. ←

I didn't think things could get worse. But they did. Today Carly blew up at me. She said she's been really patient, waiting for me to act like my old, normal self again, but she's not going to wait forever. She wanted to know why I'm doing all this strange stuff, like wearing nail polish and talking in a phony accent. Who did I think I was, anyway?

Who <u>do</u> I think I am? I felt terrible. I <u>feel</u> terrible. I don't want to lose Carly as a friend. I told her that. I tried to explain that I was just trying out new styles, new ways of being me. She laughed and said there is only ⓄⓃⒺ way to be yourself and I used to know what that was. When I remember who I am, she said, then I can be her friend again, but right now she's tired of the non-Amelia Amelia.

Carly telling me off →

I thought I'd be blown over backward! ↙

Leah hasn't changed a bit. I even recognize the clothes she wears. And she's as neat as ever. She's the only person I know who packs a napkin and a toothbrush in her lunch — and she actually uses them!

I sat with Leah at lunch today. We haven't had lunch together for a long time. But Carly's mad at me, and ther' never any room to sit next to Charisse, so when I saw an empty place near Leah, I took it. She said I seemed different to her, but she couldn't say exactly how. I asked if it was a good different or a bad different. She looked at me a long time. Then she said, "I don't kn' Did you get your hair cut?"

I wanted to scream "NO! I'm an all-new Ah-mell-ya more charming and wonderful than the old A-meal-ia." B' if I have to say that, then I guess I'm not acting like an all-new person, but the same-old, same-old. Except to Carly, who thinks I'm not the old Amelia, but not an improvement, either.

To Carly, I'm the non-Amelia Amelia. That sounds terrible, like a big, fat zero.

or a generic, bland Amelia with all the personality erased

no favorite foods, like cold pizza and pickles (but not cold pickle pizza)

no familiar habits

like racing b' slippers aroun' room

Arf!

no drawing or writing — in notebooks, on homework, on mom's shopping list

no quirky nam' for things, like calling poodles "ploo'"

I **LOVE** getting mail, and getting mysterious packages is the best!

Just when I thought nothing could go right, I got a package in the mail. It was from Mako, my pen pal. Before opening it, I carefully took off the stamps to save them because Japanese stamps are always so beautiful.

How come American stamps aren't this cute?

I love Mako! He sends the best things and writes great letters, too. This time he wrote to me about Girls' Day, when beautiful dolls are displayed in people's homes to make girls' wishes come true. There is a Boys' Day, too, also with dolls, but the boys have carp streamers and the girls don't. (I don't know why.)

The streamers look like fish flags flapping in the wind. Mako drew me a picture, which I'm copying here. It reminds me of Nadia's fish. I'm getting a lot of fish in the mail lately. Does that mean something's fishy?

Because I'm a girl, he sent me seven little dolls. They're the Seven Gods of Luck, so maybe they'll bring me good fortune. Maybe my wishes will finally come true — Charisse will like me, and Carly will stop being mad at me.

The Seven Gods of Luck —
they've already brought me some good luck!
This is the first careful drawing I've done
in a loooooong time. It took forever,
but it was worth it because now I can
keep my luck in my notebook.

I have a great idea! I may not have a Pocket Pal, but I've got a pocket do<u>ll</u>. I can put a little lucky god in my pocket each day. And since there are seven of them, I'll have one for each day of the week.

It worked! My luck has changed! I found a real treasure at the dig today. At first I thought it was just a weed, stuck in the dirt. But how could a weed be so far beneath the ground? I wondered. I carefully scraped around it, and the weed became a bunch of weeds. Only they weren't weeds at all — they were strands of plants woven into a basket! When I carefully lifted the whole thing out, I could see that even though it was only part of a basket, there were different colors on it. The colors

"weeds"

dirt

made a pattern — another thing that could help Professor Vallejo understand which tribe lived here. Best of all, even dirty it was beautiful.

Maybe it had handles, maybe not - we just can't tell.

This is what I found.

Maybe a girl made the basket, maybe someone just like me.

This is how big the whole thing probably was.

I'm drawing her with braids, but I don't really know how she wore her hair.

I couldn't believe it! I was actually holding in my hands something a Native American had made hundreds of years ago! Some woman had carefully gathered reeds and woven them together to make it. Then she had probably carried grain in it and fed her family from it. This basket was part of someone's life! And whoever made it was an artist, weaving designs into the basket to make it special. I wanted to keep it, but I knew I had to give it to Professor Vallejo. Everything we find will go on display at the local history museum.

Before I gave my basket up, I wanted to show EVERYBODY! I thought Charisse would be as excited— I mean, I was _her_ partner — so I showed her first. But she wasn't excited at all, just relieved.

All she said was, "Good! We've finally found something. Now we can stop looking and get away from all this dreadful dust." But I didn't want to stop. I wanted to find more things. Maybe there was another basket nearby, or parts of this one, just waiting for me to discover them.

I didn't want to join the crowd showing stuff to Professor Vallejo. My basket felt too special for that.

I wanted to run and show Carly, but then I remembered that she was still mad at me. So I just stood there a minute looking at my basket myself. I should have been really happy, really excited. And I was. But if Carly had been happy and excited with me, then things would have been perfect.

"Well, what are you waiting for?" Charisse asked. "Don't you need to turn that thing in?"

She was right. There was no reason to keep the basket anymore. So I plowed through all the kids around the professor and gave it to her. I didn't even wait for her to say "Good work." All I could think about was Carly.

I thought if I rubbed my lucky god, maybe it would bring me luck with her, but when I reached into my shirt pocket, it was GONE!

I may have found a basket, but I lost my lucky god. I looked for it EVERYWHERE! No luck. Of course, no luck. How could I have good luck without it?

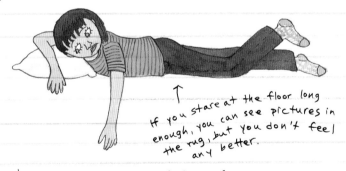

↑
If you stare at the floor long enough, you can see pictures in the rug, but you don't feel any better.

I spent the rest of the afternoon on my bed, thinking. Maybe Carly's right. I thought I was just trying to improve myself, but all this stuff is getting in the way of what I already do well (what I used to do well). I haven't been drawing or writing stories. I'm not a good friend to Charisse OR to Carly. I'm not doing ANYTHING right anymore.

I really owed Carly an apology. She was right all along.

At dinner, Mom actually called me Ah-mell-ya. I'd given up hope she'd ever get my name right, but now when I've decided I like A-meal-ia better, she says Ah-mell-ya. I told her that was just a trial period and I'm really A-meal-ia, like she's called me since I was a baby. I thought she'd be happy, but she went off on one of her long Mom-isms.

Once Mom starts on one of these, I just nod my head every so often and TUNE OUT.

That's perfect! Just perfect! Here I bend over backward to do what you want, after all the times you've insisted on Ah-mell-ya, and finally I remember to say it the way you want, but do I get any thanks? Do I get any appreciation? Of course not!

← Forget it, mom — just eat your noodles!

Then Cleo started in. It was a terrible dinner.

So your big self-improvement kick is over? That's a relief! It's no improvement to try to be something you're not.

cleo pretending to give me sisterly advice

Noodles were flying everywhere.

I try not to look at Cleo when she's talking at dinner. Who wants to see chewed-up food?

At recess the next day I went up to Carly and said I was sorry for acting like such a goof. I told her I was finished trying on styles, since none of them fit. I'm ready to be me again. Most of all, I'm ready to be her friend. I missed her terribly even though she was right in front of me.

Luckily Carly forgave me — even without my lucky god.

No more Ah-mell-ya?

DEFINITELY NOT!

← same face

← same voice

see — no more nail polish! →

I guess I <u>have</u> changed after all — I've changed my mind about myself.

I had to tell Nadia there was no all-new me in case she was expecting some amazing transformation. I wrote her a letter (a looong letter) about Charisse and Carly and all the stupid things I tried. (I hope she doesn't think I'<u>m</u> stupid, too.) I felt a <u>lot</u> better once I got that letter out. Writing always does that for me — I'd forgotten how much it helps.

stamps for Nadia letters ↘

No matter what, I promised myself I'd <u>never</u> stop writing and drawing again. They're <u>much</u> too important parts of myself to lose.

rooster ← stamp

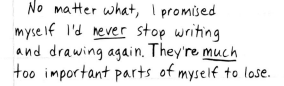

COCK O' DOODLE 12¢

At the dig, I didn't even try to be nice to Charisse. I mean, I wasn't **mean**, I was my regular self nice, not that fake, super-sweet, nicey-nice nice. And Charisse didn't seem to mind. At least, she didn't act any different, and I felt 𝒫𝒪𝒩𝒮 better because I could relax and just be me.

It's funny, but worrying about acting the right way around Charisse made me all stiff, like I was walking with a book on my head that could fall off any minute.

Now, I feel like I can turn cartwheels!

Before it felt like I was walking on eggs.

Oops! One cracked!

Now it's like I'm on a carpet of daisies!

Interesting find! It looks like a small sculpture, perhaps honoring a great person.

So that part was better, but I still didn't find my lucky god. You would think that if I could find stuff from a hundred years ago, I could find something from a few days ago! It'll probably take an archaeologist decades from now to discover it.

↑Maybe there'll be a parade with confetti.

Ms. Busby made an announcement on Friday. We had worked really hard on the excavation and so had lots of other kids. Now our time was up, and the city wanted to thank us. We were all invited to a celebration on Monday. The mayor would be there, and a band, and we would all get an official certificate for doing our part.

The certificate would probably look like this. ↓

This Certificate is Awarded to
_____
for participating in the
important historical work
of archaeological excavation.

Blah Blah
MAYOR

Yak Yak
TREASURER

I was so excited! I couldn't wait for Monday! (Usually, it's Friday I'm eager for, not Monday.)

I wrote to Mako (I'm in a writing mood lately) and told him about all the work we'd done. I promised to send him a photo so he can see the basket I found. And I thanked him for the seven lucky gods. I said a lucky god had even helped me find my basket. I didn't tell him it was lost now — that would be bad luck. Anyway, even with only six gods, I still feel lucky.

On Monday, no one could settle down, we were so eager for the celebration. Finally it was time to go, and we all started walking to the dig. I wanted to go with Carly, but Ms. Busby paired us with our work partners, so I had to walk with Charisse. Not that I don't like Charisse, but now that Carly's not mad at me, I really wanted to be with her. I didn't want her to think I liked Charisse more!

Carly is *so* great! It's like she knew what I was thinking. She was walking in front of me, but she turned back and gave me a wink.

It was like a secret signal that we were still friends.

The celebration was terrific. The mayor was there, there were lots of speeches (well, *that* part was boring), and reporters from a local TV station interviewed people and took pictures. It felt very important, but there was a fun part, too, with the band playing music and cookies and punch and *lots* of balloons.

There was a big balloon arch over the stage.

Everyone got a certificate just like Ms. Busby said we would. I'm putting mine on my bulletin board.

But the best part was a complete surprise. Just when the last kid had been given a certificate, the owner of the lot came onstage to talk.

Ahem... I want to congratulate you on all your hard work. I'm very impressed by what you've discovered.

In fact, I'm so impressed that I've decided to delay construction for a year to give you the chance to fully excavate this historical site.

The crowd went wild! Everyone cheered and whistled and clapped. A crowd of reporters mobbed the owner, and the band started playing a polka. It was great!

I was drinking punch with Carly, looking at the display of all the things we found, when Charisse came up to me. She looked right at me, plain old Amelia, not the all-new, improved kind, and she gave me a big smile. I couldn't believe it!

Oh, Ah-mell-ya, isn't it <u>wonderful</u> to see our basket on display like this? I'm <u>so</u> proud!

It's by far the best thing that's been found, don't you agree? Terrific job, Ah-mell-ya!

Pocket skunk

Charisse was <u>so</u> friendly. I kept thinking, This is it, this is what you wanted. But I didn't care about Charisse anymore. I mean, she's nice, but she's no Carly.

What I really wanted to do was show Carly my find. And I wanted to do it without Charisse. I wasn't rude or anything. I just smiled back and said, "Yeah, good work." And when Charisse went to get some more punch, I took Carly to show her the basket. It <u>did</u> look beautiful, especially now that it was all cleaned up.

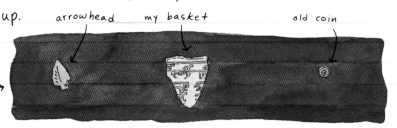

part of the display of things we found →

arrowhead   my basket   old coin

Carly loved it. I do, too. It still feels like <u>my</u> basket somehow. Carly said it was cool that I was probably the first person to see it in 100 years. I hadn't thought about that!

After seeing my basket, Carly said she'd found a treasure, too. She reached in her pocket and pulled out my lucky god.

My lucky god was in good hands all along!

I couldn't believe it! We both started talking at once, me telling how I looked for it EVERYWHERE, her telling how it must have rolled down the slope and into the pit where she was digging. Since it had gotten dirty, she thought it was something that had been buried for a while. (But she knew it wasn't ancient or she would have turned it in to Professor Vallejo.)

I couldn't stop grinning. "I guess my lucky god knew who my true friend was all the time."

It was lucky that the god got lost after all, because it brought me luck with Carly forgiving me.

Carly and I walked home together, just like old times. It had been a **PERFECT** day — the celebration, finding my lucky god, and best of all, being with my best friend again. Everything felt just right, even being me in my old, comfortable way.

And **FINALLY** I felt like writing a story again.

No one tells knock-knock jokes like Carly. ↓

plain old Amelia, just the way I like it ↓

Knock knock.

Who's there?

I. Gotta.

I. Gotta who?

I Gotta be meeee!

ordinary backpack, not a satchel ↓

no Pocket Pet

← Holding a colored pen in my hand felt so much more natural to me than having colors on my fingers!

THE WHO ? AM I STORY

by ? who did you say?

There once was a girl who grew up without ever once seeing herself in a mirror. She had no idea what she looked like. She only knew what she felt like, from the inside out. She didn't know how her voice sounded to other people, she only knew how it sounded to herself. And she was happy that way until one day she went to a carnival and saw all the fun-house mirrors.

She saw herself stretched out, squashed down, pulled sideways, and all wiggly-waggly.

Is this me?
↓

Or this?
↓

Or this?
↓

Nothing she saw matched how she saw herself in her head. It was like a nightmare! Who was she really? She couldn't tell. She didn't know anymore.

She decided she needed to find a regular mirror, not a fun-house one. Then she would see what she looked like. She would know who she was. By the Guess Your Weight game there was an ordinary mirror. She was nervous, but she went up to it and saw a girl looking back at her. She looked into the girl's eyes and smiled a big smile. There she was — herself. And she liked what she saw.

~ The End ~

me again

inside and out!